For my darling kai

www.randomhouse.com/kids

ISBN: 0-375-82410-3

Library of Congress Control Number: 2002106696

PRINTED IN BELGIUM

10 9 8 7 6 5 4 3 2 1

First American Edition

The Lonesome Polar Bear

by Jane Cabrera

Random House New York

There once was a lonesome polar bear whose only friend was a fluffy white snow cloud.

He loved the cloud,
but he wished for a friend
he could play with.

The snow cloud felt sorry for
the polar bear, so he decided to
make him a friend.
Very carefully, he dropped
snowflakes down into the shape
of an owl.
The polar bear was very happy.
"Maybe he will play with me,"
he thought.

So the polar bear threw a snowball
at the owl. It landed with a soft
squelch on its head. But the owl did
not move or hoot because it was only
made of snow.

The next day it had melted away.

The snow cloud tried again.
This time he made a big whale.
"Maybe we can swim and splash
together," thought the polar bear.

So the polar bear jumped into
the water and swam toward the
whale. But it just floated away
without a sound. The next day
the whale had melted away.

The snow cloud tried again. This time he made a seal. The polar bear took her a fish as a present.

"Maybe she will be my friend," he thought.

But snow seals don't eat fish, so the polar bear sadly took the fish away and ate it on his own. The next day the snow seal had melted away.

The snow cloud tried one last time.
He dropped snowflakes slowly down
into the shape of a reindeer.

"Perhaps she will play hide-and-seek
with me," the polar bear thought, and
off he went to hide.

The polar bear hid for a long time. But the reindeer never moved. He knew that like all his other snow friends, the reindeer would just melt away.

The next day, as the sun rose, he saw another polar bear. "He won't be real," he thought sadly. "He'll just be made of snow."

He was just about to walk away
when a snowflake drifted slowly
down onto the snow polar bear's nose.
And the snow polar bear . . .

let out an enormous sneeze . . .

ACHOO!

"You're real!" gasped the polar bear. "Will you play with me?" And he did! They played tag and hide-and-seek, and the snow cloud dropped snowflakes for them to chase. And the lonesome polar bear wasn't lonesome anymore.